Pink & Blue Punks

{ NICE TO READ YOU! }

Pink & Blue Punks

Telma Guimarães

Ilustrações de Weberson Santiago

© Editora do Brasil S.A., 2014
Todos os direitos reservados
Texto © Telma Guimarães
Ilustrações © Weberson Santiago

DIREÇÃO EXECUTIVA Maria Lúcia Kerr Cavalcante Queiroz
DIREÇÃO EDITORIAL Cibele Mendes Curto Santos
GERÊNCIA EDITORIAL Felipe Ramos Poletti
SUPERVISÃO DE ARTE E EDITORAÇÃO Adelaide Carolina Cerutti
SUPERVISÃO DE CONTROLE DE PROCESSOS EDITORIAIS Marta Dias Portero
SUPERVISÃO DE DIREITOS AUTORAIS Marilisa Bertolone Mendes
SUPERVISÃO DE REVISÃO Dora Helena Feres
EDIÇÃO Gilsandro Vieira Sales
ASSISTÊNCIA EDITORIAL Flora Vaz Manzione
AUXÍLIO EDITORIAL Paulo Fuzinelli
COORDENAÇÃO DE ARTE Maria Aparecida Alves
PRODUÇÃO DE ARTE Obá Editorial
 COORDENAÇÃO Simone Oliveira
 EDIÇÃO Mayara Menezes do Moinho
 PROJETO GRÁFICO E DIAGRAMAÇÃO Thaís Gaal Rupeika
COORDENAÇÃO DE REVISÃO Otacilio Palareti
REVISÃO Equipe EBSA
CONTROLE DE PROCESSOS EDITORIAIS Leila P. Jungstedt e Bruna Alves

DADOS INTERNACIONAIS DE CATALOGAÇÃO NA PUBLICAÇÃO (CIP)
(CÂMARA BRASILEIRA DO LIVRO, SP, BRASIL)

Andrade, Telma Guimarães Castro
 Pink & blue punks/Telma Guimarães;
ilustrações de Weberson Santiago. – 2. ed. –
São Paulo: Editora do Brasil, 2014. – (Nice to read you!)

 ISBN 978-85-10-05470-6

1. Inglês (Ensino fundamental) I. Santiago,
Weberson. II. Título. III. Série.

14-05271   CDD-372.652

ÍNDICES PARA CATÁLOGO SISTEMÁTICO:
1. Inglês : Ensino fundamental   372.652

2ª edição / 5ª impressão, 2024
Impresso na Forma Certa Gráfica Digital.

Avenida das Nações Unidas, 12901
Torre Oeste, 20º andar
São Paulo, SP – CEP: 04578-910
Fone: + 55 11 3226-0211
www.editoradobrasil.com.br

The girls were chatting.

Then I heard Susie saying: "Look at Vivian's haircut! She's so envious! She went to my hairdresser and asked him to cut her hair just like mine!"

Why do we all have to dress the same way? Why do we think it's wonderful if people have the same hairdo?

There were a lot of questions in my mind. Questions with no answers. My biggest question at that moment was, "Why did my parents make me like this?"

I wish I had been born with normal hair. I look like a porcupine. My best friends have curly hair or straight hair.

Why don't parents ask us how we would like to be before we are born?

I wish I had been born with straight hair. Every morning I get into a fight with my hair in front of the mirror. It's awful.

Nobody wants hair like mine. I'd rather not have any hair problems, like Susie.

"Hi, guys." Diana stopped and smiled at me.

"Hi." That's all I could answer.

I felt stupid. In fact, I was too shy. I couldn't talk to girls. They were always laughing and I was sure it was about my hair.

That day, during English class, the teacher asked us to write a composition called "I wish I were…"

Nothing came to my mind.

Suddenly, it occurred to me that I could do something different. Something to get the girls' attention. I would try out an experiment as soon as I got home. Maybe my mother could help me. I would probably get the girls' attention.

I wrote my composition and handed it in to the teacher. It was called "Pink Punk".

I went home with a strange feeling. A feeling of change.

"Mom, would you read this magazine article, please?" I asked. "It says you can dye your hair with colored paper and warm water. Do we have any colored paper here at home?" I was getting excited.

"Maybe pink."

She opened one of her desk drawers.

"Would you mind dyeing my hair pink?" I was a little embarrassed to ask.

"What for?" she asked. She was getting curious.

"I don't know. Just to be different, I guess."

"Well, OK. Why not?"

That's my mom.

She read the article in my sister's magazine. It explained about dyeing hair with colored paper. It was harmless and would stay in only a few days.

She asked me to take off my white t-shirt. Then she heated up some water. I stretched out on a chair in the bathroom, wrapped a towel around my neck and laid my head back.

"Just sit nice and quiet now, Tom", she said.

After a while I asked "How's it going?"

"I'm doing my best", she said while she wet the paper with warm water. Then she kept on wetting my hair. "I think it's turning pink!", she said.

"Don't you think we should have used green?" I was worried.

"You would look like 'The Incredible Hulk'," she laughed. "I hope this dye isn't too hard to get out."

After she had finished, she brought me the mirror. Wow! My hair really looked cool! It was completely pink. And so were the towel, my back, the chair, and everything else.

"Look at the floor!" I said.

Mom didn't like what she saw.

"Go outside and let the sun dry out your hair, Tom," she said. "I don't know what your father's going to say about your hair. He'll probably think we're both nuts."

I didn't care. I was happy. I looked different. I kissed mom, but she didn't like getting pink dye on her face. It seemed I was melting.

Can you believe that my sister Julie was furious at me? She said she would never tell anybody she was my sister. I didn't mind. I was happy.

Dad didn't like it either. He said he preferred my natural color rather than pink.

But I had another problem to face. The sheets were pink, the pillow case was pink, and so were my t-shirts.

As I showered I realized I wouldn't have that color for long. It would fade a little every time I washed my hair.

I looked at myself in the mirror. I looked different. I felt different. I hated my hair, so why not make the best of something I didn't like? Why not at least turn my hair into something interesting?

The next day, my friends Mark, Bruce and Tim really liked my hair.

"Wow! That looks cool!"

"Great!"

"Terrific!"

"Where did you get it done?"

"Who dyed it?"

"Why did you do it?"

I told them I just felt like it.

Then Diana, Susie, Vivian and Martha came over. They said I was totally "cool".

"Tom, how nice that looks!"

"Is it going to stay in for good?"

"Did it cost a lot to have it done?"

"Man, you look so different!"

The rest of the kids didn't like my hair. In fact, they said they hated it. Some of

them said pink was a girl's color. They are really prejudiced!

The only teacher who said something was Mrs. Baker.

"Tom, what a charming color your hair is!" she said.

I stood up and said "Thanks, Mrs. Baker." I could hardly believe what I had done. I was the shy type. Was that me standing in front of the class and looking around?

"After class let me know what kind of dye you used, Tom. I might try it next time in my hairdresser", the teacher said.

I was surrounded by people during lunch. We were at the cafeteria, but I could hardly eat lunch.

"Disgusting."

"What a bad taste!"

"Looks too gaudy."

"Incredible!"

"I like it!"

Diana sat down at my table. I offered her some of my apple pie and she accepted. She thought I was kind of crazy for doing that to my hair. She pointed to my t-shirt and said it looked like I was melting. I agreed. It was a hot day and the next day I would wear a black t-shirt or try a better way to dye my hair.

I felt more sure of myself. I knew some people didn't like it but I wasn't worried about them. It had been a way to catch Diana's attention and I had succeeded.

I invited her to a party and she accepted.

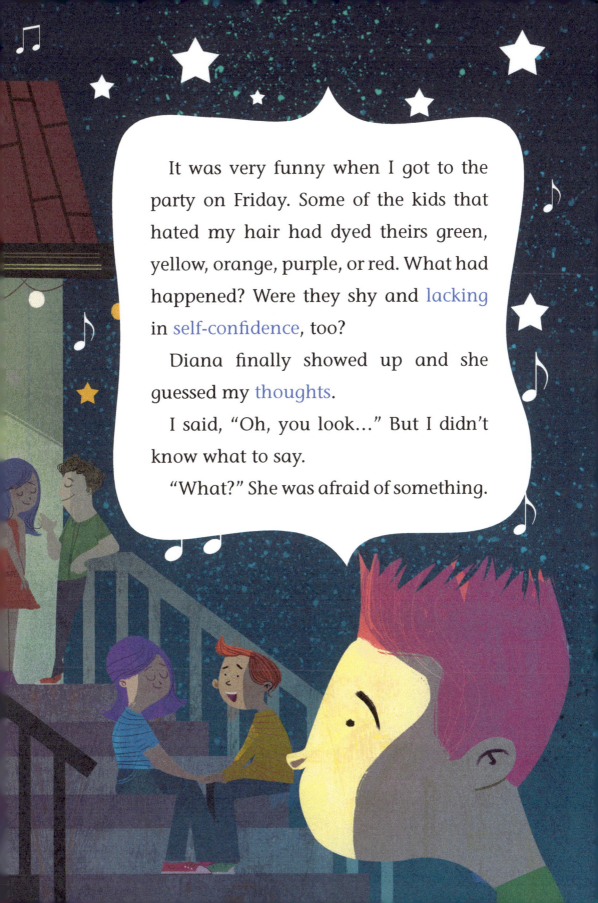

It was very funny when I got to the party on Friday. Some of the kids that hated my hair had dyed theirs green, yellow, orange, purple, or red. What had happened? Were they shy and lacking in self-confidence, too?

Diana finally showed up and she guessed my thoughts.

I said, "Oh, you look…" But I didn't know what to say.

"What?" She was afraid of something.

"Forget it." I kissed her and looked at her weird blue hair. She had dyed her beautiful black hair blue and had gotten a haircut, too. Her long hair was short now, like mine. "You look great," I told her.

In fact, she looks great anyway.

Guess what! She thinks the same about me.

The next day I heard my sister Julie talking to mom in a low voice.

"Mom, would you dye my hair blue, like Diana's? Her hair is really something," I heard her ask. "You know, she told the girls she went to a fancy hairdresser who gave her a very stylish cut. And she dyed it blue, mom. It's really something!"

Isn't that funny?

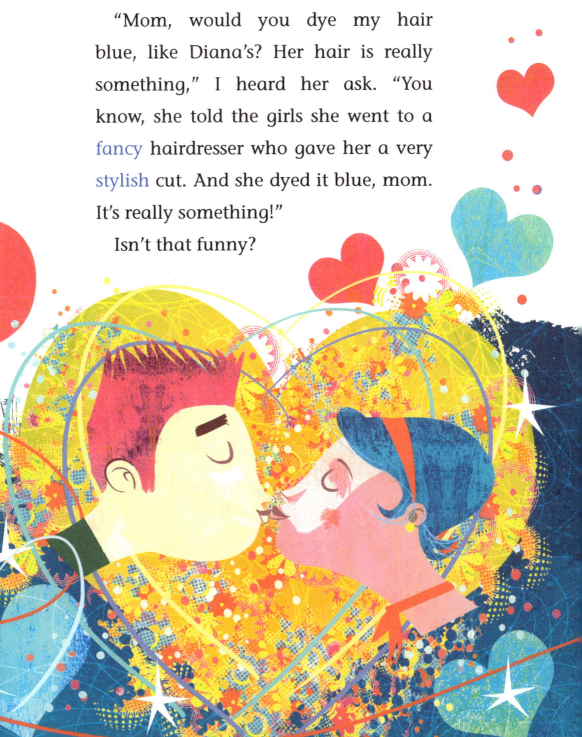

Glossary }

In alphabetical order

anyway	de qualquer jeito	**classmate**	colega de classe
as soon as	assim que, logo que	**cool**	legal
		curly	ondulado, crespo
at least	ao menos	**disgusting**	horrível
awful	horrível	**drawer**	gaveta
both	ambos(as)	**envious**	invejoso(a)
cafeteria	lanchonete, cantina	**fancy**	sofisticado(a)
		feeling	sensação; sentimento
		for good	definitivamente, para sempre
		gaudy	exagerado, espalhafatoso
		hairdo	penteado

porcupine	porco-espinho
prejudiced	preconceituoso(a)
rather than	em vez de
self-confidence	autoconfiança
sheets	lençóis
shy	tímido(a)
sneakers	tênis
straight	liso
stylish	elegante; estiloso
suddenly	de repente
surrounded	rodeado(a)
taste	gosto
terrific	sensacional
thought	pensamento
to agree	concordar
to care	importar-se
to come over	ir até o lugar em que alguém está
to dry out	secar
to dye	tingir

hairdresser	cabeleireiro(a)
harmless	inofensivo(a)
I would rather (I'd rather)	eu preferiria
look-alike	semelhante
low	baixo(a)
might	poderia
mirror	espelho
neck	pescoço
nuts	louco(a)
parents	pais
pillow case	fronha

to fade	desbotar	to look like	parecer
to feel like something	ter vontade de algo	to melt	derreter
		to mind	importar-se
to guess	achar, adivinhar	to realize	perceber, compreender
to hand in	entregar	to seem	parecer
to heat up	aquecer	to stay	ficar, permanecer
to hope	esperar	to stretch out	esticar-se
to invite	convidar	to succeed	ser bem-sucedido, sair-se bem
to keep on	continuar	to try out	experimentar
to lack	não ter, ser carente de	to wet	umedecer, molhar
to laugh	rir	to wrap	enrolar
to lay back	pôr para trás	towel	toalha
		way	modo, jeito
		weird	estranho, esquisito
		while	tempo, momento
		worried	preocupado(a)

About the author...

Telma Guimarães is a Brazilian writer of books for children and young people. She graduated in Portuguese and English, which explains why she loves writing in these languages. She loves literature and books, and she has already published a lot of good, fun, and creative stories. Telma lives in Campinas, a city in the state of São Paulo, Brazil. She is married and a mother of three kids. She also has a granddaughter, with whom she shares a lot of stories.

About the illustrator...

Weberson Santiago was born in São Bernardo do Campo, in 1983. He was raised in Mauá and lived for some time in São Paulo, but nowadays he lives in Mogi das Cruzes. Besides illustrating books, Weberson also writes. He teaches at the University of Mogi das Cruzes and at Quanta Academia de Artes.

Este livro foi composto com a família tipográfica
Stone Informal Std, para a Editora do Brasil, em maio de 2014.